Jasper an

Written by Michèle Dufresne ▪ Illustrated by Sterling Lamet

Pioneer Valley Educational Press, Inc.

"Look at the birds,"
said Katie.
"I can see yellow birds
in the tree!
They are hungry!"

2

3

Katie went into the house.

"Mom," she said.

"I can see yellow birds in the tree!

They are hungry!"

Things To Remember
Rice
Cat Food

5

"Here is some bread for the birds," said Mom. "You can feed the birds."

"Here is some bread," Katie said to the birds. "Look at the bread!"

Jasper looked
at the bread.
He looked and looked.

10

"Jasper," said Katie.
"You are a naughty cat!
The bread is
for the birds,
not for you!"